A CAT IS CHASING ME THROUGH THIS BOOK!
is published by Capstone Young Readers,
A Capstone Imprint
1710 Roe Crest Drive
North Mankato, Minnesota 56003
www.capstoneyoungreaders.com

CAPS32944

Library of Congress Cataloging-in-Publication Data
is available on the Library of Congress website.
ISBN: 978-1-62370-126-0 (paper over board)
ISBN: 978-1-4795-5229-0 (library hardcover)
ISBN: 978-1-4795-6161-2 (eBook)

DESIGNED BY:
Russell Griesmer

ILLUSTRATED BY:
Comicup Studio
Carmen Pérez – Pencils
Francesc Figueres Farrès – Inks
Gloria Caballe – Color

Printed in the United States of America in North Mankato, Minnesota.
042014 008087CGF14

A CAT IS CHASING ME THROUGH THIS BOOK!

by Benjamin Bird

CAPSTONE YOUNG READERS
capstoneyoungreaders.com

POP!

Flap, flap, flap
your arms to help me
fly across these pages!

Kick, kick, kick
your legs to help me
swim across this sea!

Stomp, stomp, stomp
your feet to get me over
this mountain!

Wiggle, wiggle, wiggle
like a worm to squeeze
through these tunnels!

CHOMP!
CHOMP!

Shoosh, shoosh, shoosh
to keep me quiet as a mouse.

Clap, clap, clap
your hands to keep away
these jungle pests!

Rub, rub, rub
your arms to keep me
warm in this snow!

Blink, blink, blink
to keep this sand out
of my eyes!

Chomp, chomp, chomp
your teeth to help me
eat my way out!

HA!
You have nowhere left to go, Jerry.
How are they going to help you now?
That's easy . . .

Whistle, whistle, whistle
to help me call a furry friend!

RUUF!
RUUF!
RUUF!

AHHH!

Wave, wave, wave
good-bye to good old Tom.